THE ARMY

DEFEND AND PROTECT

Sarah Levete

Gareth Stevens
PUBLISHING

Please visit our website, www.garethstevens.com.
For a free color catalog of all our high-quality books,
call toll free 1-800-542-2595 or fax 1-877-542-2596.

Cataloging-in-Publication Data

Levete, Sarah.
The Army / by Sarah Levete.
p. cm. — (Defend and protect)
Includes index.
ISBN 978-1-4824-4119-2 (pbk.)
ISBN 978-1-4824-4120-8 (6-pack)
ISBN 978-1-4824-4121-5 (library binding)
1. United States. — Army — Juvenile literature.
I. Levete, Sarah. II. Title.
UA25.L48 2016
355.00973—d23

First Edition

Published in 2016 by
Gareth Stevens Publishing
111 East 14th Street, Suite 349
New York, NY 10003

Produced by Calcium
Editors: Sarah Eason and Jennifer Sanderson
Designers: Paul Myerscough and Simon Borrough
Picture research: Jennifer Sanderson

Picture credits: Department of Defense (DoD): 6, 27t, CPhoM. Robert F. Sergeant 19, Fred W. Baker
III 32, 39 top, Melvin G. Tarpley 34, Petty Officer 1st Class Daniel N. Woods 9, Sgt. Cherie A. Thurlby
12, Sgt. Christopher S. Barnhart 5t, Sgt. Freddy G. Cantu 4, Sgt. Margaret Taylor, 129th Mobile Public
Affairs Detachment 13t, Sgt. Michael J. Carden 25, Spc. Daniel Love 3, 22, 23, Spc. Eric Cabra 1, 10,
Spc. Eric Cabral, 36, Tia P. Sokimson 18t, Staff Sgt. Ian Shay, Staff Sgt. Stacy L. Pearsall 28, Tech. Sgt.
Jeremy T. Lock 40, 45, Tech. Sgt. Rick Sforza 17; Dreamstime: Darrenw 5b, 11b, 15b, 18b, 27b, 33b,
39b, 43b, Yorrico 7b, 8b, 13b, 17b, 20b, 23b, 24b, 29b, 31b, 35b, 37b, 41t; Shutterstock: Hung Chung
Chih 38, Kiev.Victor 23t, Ksanawo 42b, MarKord 41b, Terry Poche 20, Vic and Julie Pigula 42–43; US
Army: Pfc. Nathaniel Newkirk 35t, Spc. Steven K. Young 30–31, Visual Information Specialist Markus
Rauchenberger 33t, Sgt. William Jones 11t; US Air Force: Tech. Sgt. Denise Rayder 26, US Marine Corps:
Lance Cpl. Jorge A. Ortiz 15t; Wikimedia Commons: Airman 1st Class Breonna Veal 21t, Sgt Steve Blake
RLC 14, US Army 29.

Printed in the United States of America

CPSIA compliance information: Batch #CW16GS: For further information contact
Gareth Stevens, New York, New York at 1-800-542-2595.

Contents

CHAPTER 1:
The Armed Forces

Who is trained to risk their life in the name of their country? Who is prepared to use weapons to defend and protect others? Who will go on long tours of duty, far from home, living in rough-and-ready conditions? The answer to all these questions is the men and women in the army.

The army is the land-based branch of the military or armed forces. The other main branches of the armed forces are the air force and navy. All areas of the armed forces work together, but each one has a separate role, and their men and women have expertise in keeping their country and people safe.

Marines in the US Navy

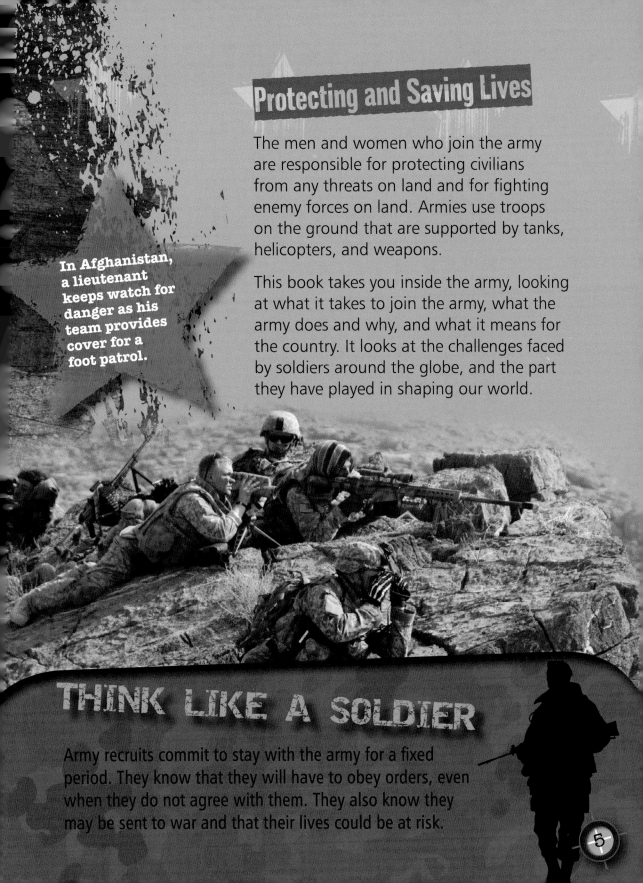

Protecting and Saving Lives

The men and women who join the army are responsible for protecting civilians from any threats on land and for fighting enemy forces on land. Armies use troops on the ground that are supported by tanks, helicopters, and weapons.

This book takes you inside the army, looking at what it takes to join the army, what the army does and why, and what it means for the country. It looks at the challenges faced by soldiers around the globe, and the part they have played in shaping our world.

In Afghanistan, a lieutenant keeps watch for danger as his team provides cover for a foot patrol.

THINK LIKE A SOLDIER

Army recruits commit to stay with the army for a fixed period. They know that they will have to obey orders, even when they do not agree with them. They also know they may be sent to war and that their lives could be at risk.

Who Joins the Army?

The men and women who join the army love the unexpected, working in different places, and having a career in which no day is the same. The army, during peacetime or a conflict, is hard work but rewarding.

An army is a huge organization. In the United States, the army is made up of more than 675,000 soldiers, with nearly 190,000 in the Army Reserve. The Army Reserve is made up of men and women who train for the army but keep their civilian jobs. They may be called to action if there is a war. Officers lead and give orders to enlisted soldiers, and are responsible for their safety. Enlisted soldiers carry out orders and perform specific duties. They can work their way up to become noncommissioned officers. People with specific qualifications and skills can join the army as commissioned officers.

Today, in many of the world's armies, women have opportunities in combat roles similar to those of male soldiers.

Rank and File

Each country's army is organized in a different way. A typical structure is:

★ **Corporal:** leads a fire team of three

★ **Sergeant**: leads a squad (up to 12 soldiers)

★ **Lieutenant:** leads a platoon (about 4 squads, up to 40 soldiers)

★ **Captain**: leads a company (about 4 platoons, 100–200 soldiers)

★ **Lieutenant Colonel**: commands a battalion or squadron (3–5 companies, up to 1,200 soldiers)

★ **Colonel:** commands a brigade or regiment (about 4 battalions, up to 5,000 soldiers)

★ **Major General:** commands a division (3 brigades, up to 18,000 soldiers)

★ **Lieutenant General:** commands a corps (2–3 divisions)

★ **General:** commands a field army (2 or more corps)

ACT LIKE A PRIVATE

Private is the lowest army rank. Privates can work their way up through the army but it takes patience and discipline. Privates have to obey all orders and answer their sergeants with a loud and clear "Sir," or "Ma'am."

TAKE THE TEST!

Could you be in the army?

Recruits who join the army have to pay attention. if they do not, they have to repeat their exercises. Try this test to check your attention to detail:

Q1. Who commands a brigade?

Q2. What is the land-based branch of the military called?

Q3. Is army life best suited to someone who likes routine or variety?

Q4. What is an Army Reserve soldier?

Q5. Is the United States Army made up of 5,000, 50,000, or more than 500,000 soldiers?

Q6. Who gives orders to an enlisted soldier?

Q7. The army stops work during peacetime. True or false?

Q8. What is a private?

ANSWERS

Q1. A colonel
Q2. The army
Q3. Variety
Q4. A trained soldier who leads a civilian life but stays ready for action
Q5. More than 500,000
Q6. An officer
Q7. False
Q8. A soldier of the lowest rank

CHAPTER 2:
Army Life

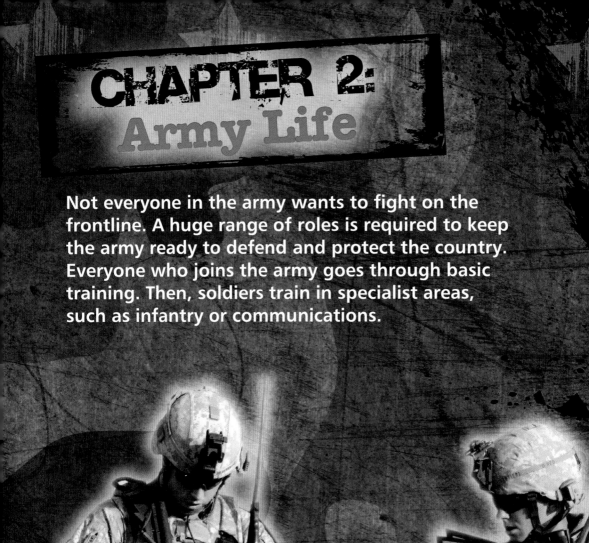

Not everyone in the army wants to fight on the frontline. A huge range of roles is required to keep the army ready to defend and protect the country. Everyone who joins the army goes through basic training. Then, soldiers train in specialist areas, such as infantry or communications.

A team of men and women support soldiers on the front line, providing weapons and food as well as data and communications.

Camping Out

An overseas army base or camp must be set up entirely from scratch. It takes many people to manage this job. The recent war in Afghanistan drew in troops from around the world to fight the Taliban. In the desert area of southern Afghanistan, British soldiers set up camp.

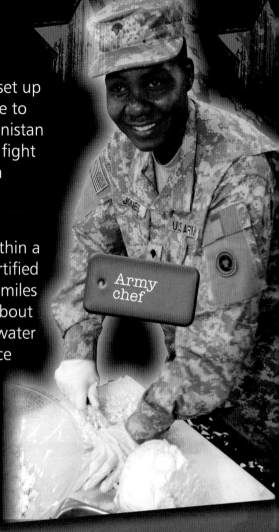

Army chef

The camp began with a few tents, but within a couple of years, it had become a huge fortified base, the size of a small town, 16 square miles (41 sq km). Camp Bastion was home to about 28,000 men and women. It had its own water bottling plant, runway, hospital, and police force. Three huge dining halls were built, each able to feed about 7,000 people. If soldiers did not want the army food, they could get a takeout from Bastion's KFC or Pizza Hut.

THINK LIKE AN ARMY CHEF

It is up to army chefs to make sure that the men and women in combat zones or in barracks are well fed. Sometimes, this means feeding hundreds of soldiers. Chefs work in well-equipped kitchens with good supplies of food. In a war zone, however, chefs must think creatively about how to use supplies to produce nourishing and energizing food for exhausted soldiers. A chef's supplies include small ration packs and pots and pans that are carried by soldiers in their backpacks.

Saving Lives

The army medical and health care team includes many roles, from dentists to veterinarians. Team members work in barracks when not on a tour of duty, and on the field during action. A team of surgeons, pharmacists, doctors, and nurses work 24 hours a day to ensure the fitness and well-being of army soldiers.

Combat medics train like any other soldiers, but they also complete medical training. Medics often come under attack, even while trying to save a wounded soldier.

Action on the front line means risk of injury or death. Emergency treatment offered by combat medics can save lives.

A Dog's World

A trained dog can search a car for explosives eight times faster than a human. Before being taken to a combat zone, dogs are trained to hunt out explosives. They are taken on helicopter rides and are exposed to the sound of gun and mortar fire so that they will not react badly when they are in a war zone. A nervous or surprised dog on the battlefield will not save lives. Army vets and dog handlers work alongside the dogs and make sure they are in the best health.

Sniffer dog

ACT LIKE A COMBAT MEDIC

During a war, combat medics live and work with the fighting troops. A medic follows every patrol, just in case it is attacked and someone is injured. Medics have to carry the basic medical kit needed to treat any injuries. They are the first on the scene when soldiers are hurt or injured. Medics deliver emergency first aid and help the seriously injured back to medical bases quickly. Medics have to perform lifesaving first aid, often under fire from the enemy, as well as figure out how to get injured soldiers out of the combat zone and to a makeshift hospital.

13

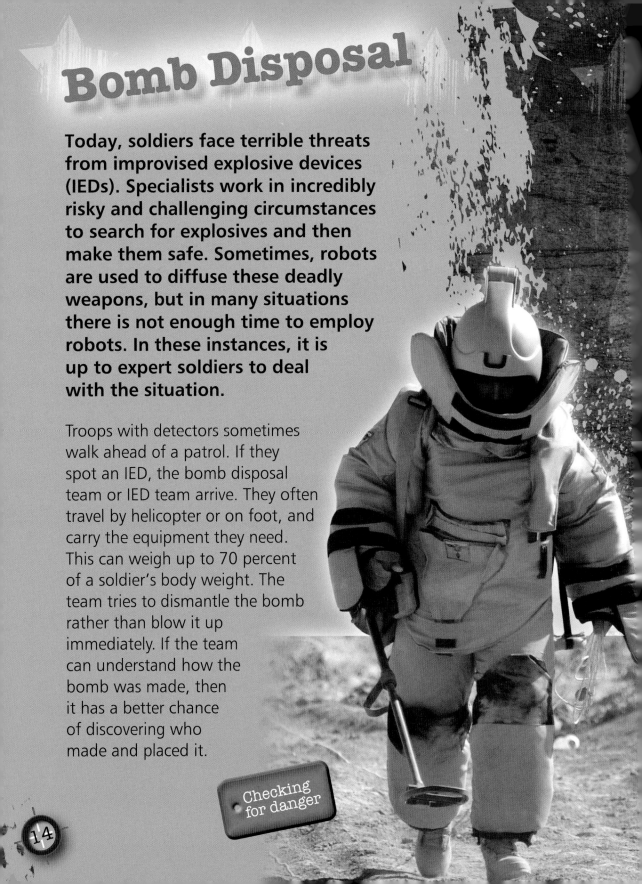

Bomb Disposal

Today, soldiers face terrible threats from improvised explosive devices (IEDs). Specialists work in incredibly risky and challenging circumstances to search for explosives and then make them safe. Sometimes, robots are used to diffuse these deadly weapons, but in many situations there is not enough time to employ robots. In these instances, it is up to expert soldiers to deal with the situation.

Troops with detectors sometimes walk ahead of a patrol. If they spot an IED, the bomb disposal team or IED team arrive. They often travel by helicopter or on foot, and carry the equipment they need. This can weigh up to 70 percent of a soldier's body weight. The team tries to dismantle the bomb rather than blow it up immediately. If the team can understand how the bomb was made, then it has a better chance of discovering who made and placed it.

Checking for danger

Watching Out

Inside trucks wrapped in special netting (to protect against rocket-propelled grenades), soldiers wear helmets, body armor, protective goggles, and strengthened underwear, while sitting on special shock-absorbing seats. From inside the armored trucks, soldiers can use long robotic metal arms to remotely inspect and check the ground for bombs.

IEDs are the main cause of casualties among troops. They kill many civilians, too.

THINK LIKE AN IED EXPERT

It is essential that IED experts think clearly under pressure, cope with heavy responsibility, and have very steady hands. Soldiers who panic will not be able to deal with the hugely stressful role undertaken by bomb disposal experts. IED experts face terrible injuries and death when diffusing devices. They must put aside any thoughts of personal risk. Instead, they must focus entirely on the device in hand.

TAKE THE TEST!

Have you learned what it takes to work in the army?

You have read about army life and the range of crucial roles played by soldiers. Do you think you could cope with the demands of working in the army? Take this test to see how well you can hold your nerve when under pressure:

Q1. What does IED stand for?

Q2. Why do IED experts try to dismantle an IED instead of blowing it up?

Q3. Why are robots not always used to detect and dismantle IEDs?

Q4. Do combat medics live separately from combat troops on a mission?

Q5. What was Camp Bastion?

Q6. How many people lived in Camp Bastion?

Q7. How do dogs get used to the noise of a helicopter?

Q8. Where does a medic treat an injured soldier?

Q1. Improvised explosive device

Q2. To try to figure out who set the device

Q3. There is not always time to arrange this

Q4. No, they live together

Q5. An army base in Afghanistan

Q6. About 28,000

Q7. By hearing the noise before being used in a conflict

Q8. On the field to give emergency first aid, and then transports the injured soldier to a makeshift hospital for additional treatment

ANSWERS

CHAPTER 3:
War and Peace

The military's key mission is to defend its country and its country's interests, but armies work on crucial peacetime missions, too. These include rescue operations and support in humanitarian disaster crises. The Indian Army even built the world's highest bridge, the Bailey Bridge in the Himalayan mountains, in 1982.

Troops at work

THINK LIKE A SOLDIER

Soldiers sign up to the army for a set period—either two or six years. Soldiers can leave if they are found unfit and cannot perform duties, or if they are unable to adapt to military life. Soldiers are expected to carry out orders during any conflict the army engages in, whether or not they agree with their country being at war.

The Cost of War

Men and women in the army know that if their country is involved in a conflict or war they will be called upon to fight. From nurses to communications experts, everyone who is sent on a mission risks injury and death.

World War II (1939–1945) led to the deaths of more than 20 million people serving in the military. About 40 million civilians died.

The Vietnam War

The Vietnam War took place from 1954 to 1975 between North Vietnam and the United States and South Vietnam. The war was fought in unknown, hostile territory. More than 58,000 men and women from the United States armed forces lost their lives in the war. US troops were unprepared for fighting in the hot and humid conditions of the dense North Vietnamese jungle. Many soldiers became unhappy with the huge loss of life suffered by their comrades, and the length of the war against a seemingly unconquerable enemy. An estimated 5 percent of soldiers deserted the army during the war.

Peacetime

Even during peacetime, the army is still active. Most armies play key roles in disaster relief. They respond to an emergency by providing men and women to organize and distribute aid, medical support, and practical support in getting people to safety and helping to restore essential services.

Hurricane Katrina

On August 29, 2005, Hurricane Katrina smashed along the north-central Gulf Coast near New Orleans, causing havoc. Land and homes were flooded. More than 1,300 people died in the disaster, covering an area almost the size of United Kingdom. Chaos followed as nearly 5 million people were left without electrical power. The US Army helped evacuate civilians stranded in the flooded areas, and deliver essential supplies of food and water. Army engineers helped drain the flooded city and repair the drains to keep it dry.

Disaster relief

Ebola

The spread of the deadly Ebola virus led to thousands of deaths across several West African countries. The US Army sent a team to Liberia to set up Ebola treatment units, training stations for local Liberian health workers, and a 25-bed hospital. The US Army Medical Research Institute of Infectious Diseases (USAMRIID) played a key role.

Troops practice putting on protective clothing before they are sent to help in countries affected by Ebola.

ACT LIKE A SOLDIER

In April 2015, an earthquake rocked Nepal. Thousands of people were killed, injured, and made homeless. The Nepalese Army went into action to rescue survivors, clear collapsed buildings, and help the battered country recover. The men and women in the army had to put aside fears and anxiety about their own loved ones as they carried out their crucial roles.

21

Special Ops

Exceptional soldiers who have passed through basic army training and are working in the army may join the elite teams of the military, known as Special Forces. These teams test and train recruits to the highest level. Only a few make it through to qualify.

Green Berets

US Special Forces are known as the Green Berets. The men who wear the green beret have been through a training course that only a handful successfully complete. The first stage pushes recruits to the limit. During this, the men must swim and run in full kit. The second phase adds treacherous and exhausting obstacle courses that recruits must complete on only a few hours sleep. Those who make it this far then have to show they have the mental and physical ability to survive in an emergency. Training prepares them to avoid capture, to resist giving in to the enemy, and to escape.

Looking for the enemy

Foreign Legion

The French Foreign Legion is the French Army's elite force. It is open to anyone of any nationality between the ages of 17 and 40. Recruits must have a valid passport and must pass a security check. Applicants must be physically fit and have medical records that prove they are in good health. There are no weight or height restrictions, but applicants must be of a healthy weight—they cannot be over or underweight.

After training, successful Legionnaires receive a hat called a "kepi blanc."

ACT LIKE AN ELITE SOLDIER

Pictures of China's secretive army show some of its elite frontline soldiers in training. This is no ordinary training. The men are wearing only combat trousers but are knee-deep in freezing snow. In temperatures of -4° Fahrenheit (-20° C), they practice their sabre (large knife) skills without flinching in the cold.

TAKE THE TEST!

Can you cope under pressure?

Soldiers must turn their hands to whatever needs to be done in an emergency. Can you cope with the pressure of this quiz?

Q1. What did the Indian Army build?

Q2. Why did so many soldiers desert the army during the Vietnam War?

Q3. Who can join the French Foreign Legion?

Q4. Who are the Green Berets?

Q5. Give one example of the US Army's peacetime activity.

Q6. How many men and women from the US armed forces lost their lives in the Vietnam War?

Q7. Can soldiers leave the army whenever they want?

Q8. In 2015, why was the Nepalese Army deployed in its home country?

25

ANSWERS

CHAPTER 4:
Training

At any time, soldiers might find themselves trekking across rugged mountains through enemy territory, working in scorching temperatures to deliver aid packages, or carrying a wounded comrade to safety. Excellent fitness is essential for these challenging situations. The tough army training begins when men and women apply to join. It continues throughout their career to ensure they are fit enough to carry out their tasks.

Hard work and discipline help recruits overcome the obstacles they face in training.

Basic army training focuses on physical and practical skills, and making sure trainees have the right attitude to become a reliable member of the army. Training is often known as "boot camp," during which recruits have to prove their physical fitness. They also have to show they can follow orders and work together as a team. Drill sergeants constantly bark instructions and criticisms. The idea is to make sure that recruits can follow orders. This is crucial in highly stressful and chaotic situations during war.

A Long, Hard Day

A typical day starts with a 4 a.m. wake up. Barracks must be tidied and cleaned. By 5 a.m., recruits are running and working out. After a quick breakfast, training continues. This might be learning to fire weapons, outdoor survival, and map reading skills. There is a short time after dinner to wind down before getting ready for more training the next day.

Morning workout

ACT LIKE A TRAINEE

At the start of training, new recruits hand over their personal belongings and are issued with army kit. Home for the next few weeks is the barracks, which recruits are expected to keep thoroughly clean. Recruits have to follow a "drill." The drill sergeant barks instructions that must be followed and pushes recruits to the limit, physically and mentally.

Fit for Purpose

From push-ups to sit-ups, trainees have to show physical fitness and mental aptitude for the job. While in the army, recruits continue to train and to prepare for the call to war. The army rehearses conflict scenarios to make sure its soldiers are best prepared for any real-life conflicts.

This exhausted but determined US Army recruit is in the final three-week phase of basic combat training.

On a mission, a soldier will need to lift a heavy survival kit and ammunition onto an army truck. One exercise given to improve recruits' strength is called the Jerry Can Carry. Trainees carry two jerry cans (water containers) each weighing 44 pounds (20 kg) over a total distance of 394 feet (120 m) in fewer than 2 minutes. A can must be held in each hand, with the soldiers' arms by their sides.

Army Values

As well as practical training in an individual's chosen role in the army, each army teaches recruits to follow the army's values. The US Army values are:

★ Loyalty ★ Duty ★ Respect   Selfless service ★ Honor
★ Integrity (knowing what is right and wrong)   Personal courage

Training is tough

THINK LIKE A DRILL SERGEANT

The job of a drill sergeant is to turn civilians into soldiers. The drill sergeant has to be tough on the recruits to make sure they will survive. The trainees will learn all that they know about the army from their drill sergeant.

TAKE THE TEST!

Do you have
what it takes?

Only the committed can cope with the army's tough training. Now it is your turn to prove you have what it takes. Check your skills on this test:

Q1. Name two of the US Army's values.

Q2. What is a jerry can?

Q3. Why is the jerry can exercise used?

Q4. What is the job of a drill sergeant?

Q5. Why does the army rehearse conflict scenarios?

Q6. Trainees can get up at any time. True or false?

Q7. What are barracks?

Q8. Boot camp is where the soldiers' boots are kept and cleaned. True or false?

ANSWERS

Q8. False. It is the informal name for the army-training period
Q7. Where recruits live and train to join the army
Q6. False. They are woken early for the start of the day
Q5. To make sure its men and women are best prepared for any real-life conflicts
Q4. To turn civilians into soldiers
Q3. To improve recruits' strength so they become used to carrying heavy loads
Q2. A water container
Q1. Any of: loyalty, duty, respect, selfless service, honor, integrity, personal courage

CHAPTER 5: Army Gear

During a conflict, soldiers might face sophisticated weapons or random homemade devices like IEDs. The US Army has an armory of powerful weapons, from grenades to heavy machine guns. Armored fighting vehicles are equipped with protection against hostile attacks and often have weapons attached.

Air and Land

Stryker combat vehicles provide armored protection against rocket-propelled grenades, and are fitted with a mobile gun system. Special army aircraft can carry up to seven Strykers to soldiers in the field. The Lockheed Martin SMSS is an 11-foot (3.4 m) unmanned vehicle that can carry up to 0.6 tons (0.5 tonnes) of a squad's equipment, including food, water, and heavy weapons. The US Army used these vehicles to cross the rugged terrain in Afghanistan.

Strykers can transport troops and provide covering fire.

Apache attack helicopters fly night and day, no matter the weather. An Apache can detect and identify up to 256 possible targets in seconds. Rockets, missiles, and other weapons are carried on board.

Nuclear Threat

In 1945, the United States dropped two nuclear weapons on the Japanese cities of Hiroshima and Nagasaki. These bombs forced the Japanese to surrender, and brought World War II to a close. However, tens of thousands of people were killed or suffered horrific long-term effects as a result of the bombs. Since then, no nation has used a nuclear bomb, although some countries, including the United States and Pakistan, have nuclear weapons.

Squad automated weapon

THINK LIKE A SOLDIER

Soldiers need nerves of steel to hold the powerful M240 as they patrol through enemy territory. This machine gun can fire 100 rounds of bullets in 1 minute. It is a killing machine. Soldiers must pull the trigger only when needed, and it must be used only against the enemy, not innocent civilians.

Survival Kit

In war, combat soldiers face enemy gunfire, missile attacks, and randomly placed IEDs. They are in constant danger. Their kit can be the difference between life and death.

Gillie suits are heavy camouflage outfits, usually worn by marksmen. The suits are covered with artificial plants that behave like real plants in the wind and rain. This helps conceal marksmen from the enemy. Scientists have developed a new type of body armor called combat body armor. It has ceramic plates to provide extra protection for soldiers. Although heavier than usual body armor, it can be fitted with pouches to carry everything from ammunition to first aid kits.

A thick gillie suit is hot and heavy to wear, but it gives realistic cover for soldiers because the enemy mistakes the fake green plants for real vegetation.

Kitted Out

Typical kit for frontline soldiers includes:

★ Special underwear that can be worn comfortably for months at a time because soldiers may not be able to take a shower

★ Sandals in which a soldier can take a quick shower but can also run for cover from enemy fire

★ Helmet fitted with night vision goggles

★ First aid kit

★ 24 hours' worth of rations

★ Compass

★ Drinking water pack

Night vision goggles

THINK LIKE A SOLDIER

It has been a long tour of duty. The soldiers' new boots no longer gleam. They are covered in dust and dirt. The soldiers are working in blazing temperatures and are mentally and physically exhausted. However, whatever the challenges faced by soldiers, they always need to make sure that the backpack, the Modular Lightweight Load-Carrying Equipment (MOLLE), they are carrying is packed with its lifesaving equipment. Failure to do so could result in death—either their own or that of a comrade.

TAKE THE TEST!

Could you cope with army kit and weapons?

Soldiers need to be prepared to use their equipment quickly and effectively. Could you remember how to handle your army kit?

Q1. How many possible targets can an Apache helicopter detect and identify in seconds?

Q2. What is a Stryker?

Q3. Who drives the Lockheed Martin SMSS?

Q4. What is a MOLLE?

Q5. Why are soldiers on some missions equipped with special underpants?

Q6. Where did the United States drop two nuclear bombs during World War II?

Q7. What does a Gillie suit do?

Q8. How many rounds of bullets can the M240 fire in one minute?

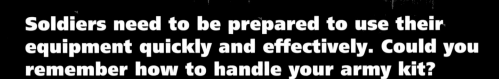

ANSWERS

Q8. 100
Q7. Help hide a soldier from enemy view
Q6. The Japanese cities of Hiroshima and Nagasaki
Q5. Because they may not have access or time to take a shower for long periods
Q4. A US Army backpack
Q3. No one. It is remotely controlled
Q2. A type of armored combat vehicle
Q1. 256

CHAPTER 6:
Around the World

China and the United States have the largest armies, and India the third largest. Moldova and Monaco have some of the smallest armies in the world. Most countries have an army but some, such as Costa Rica, choose not to. Armies from different countries often work together to keep the peace in troubled areas.

China's People's Liberation Army has 850,000 soldiers. The country's navy has 235,000, and there are 398,000 in its air force.

No Army

In 1948, the president of Costa Rica, José Figueres Ferrer, bashed a hole in the wall of the country's military headquarters with a large sledgehammer. His action showed the world that Costa Rica was getting rid of its military. He handed the keys of the headquarters to the minister of education, announcing that it would become a national art museum, and the nation's military budget would go toward health care, education, and environmental protection. To this day, Costa Rica does not have an army.

An Indian soldier trains with the US Army

At a Cost

For every conflict or war, men and women lose their lives and can suffer terrible injuries. Fighting a war may change the course of history, but it also has a terrible impact on the men and women on all sides. The financial cost of keeping an army, and other branches of the military such as the navy, is huge. Figures from 2012 showed that the United States spent $711 billion on defense, which was more than any other country.

THINK LIKE A PEACEKEEPER

A tour of duty for a soldier on a peacekeeping mission often involves working with other armies and men and women from very different backgrounds. The atmosphere is often tense as the soldiers try to keep opposing sides apart. The threat of danger is ever-present as soldiers risk attack from all parties involved in the fragile peace.

War on Terror

An army is a powerful organization with well-trained soldiers and dangerous weaponry. It is essential that an army is organized and checked to make sure individuals work to defend and protect the interests of their country, not the interests of just a few. An armed group, however, has no such structure and does not have to justify its actions to a government. In some parts of the world, armed groups pressurize children to fight for them. These young children are then forced to carry out terrible deeds.

Armies are often active in their own country, defending it from terrorist threats. The Kenyan Army is struggling to cope with the threat from the extremist group al-Shabaab. This group is responsible for many recent killings in Kenya, including an attack on a university campus in which 147 people were killed.

Different armies can share their expertise and skills. Here, US soldiers help train Kenyan soldiers.

THINK LIKE A COUNTERINTELLIGENCE OFFICER

It is essential to stop the enemy from discovering the army's plans. A counterintelligence officer makes sure that computer systems are secure. During a conflict, civilians who work on an army base must be checked to make sure they are not passing information to the enemy.

Terrorism

The world faces increasing threats from extremist groups. Armies work alongside other branches of the armed forces to counter the danger from these groups. Special Forces units are often important in this. In Afghanistan, the United States and British armies tackled the threat of terrorism with direct action, attacking the Taliban. The armies also tried to win over local people, persuading them not to support the terrorists. They did this by helping build up the local area with essential services such as medical care and education. Could this be the way forward for armies to defeat the terrorist threat?

On alert

Changing History

The success and failure of wars and conflicts have shaped our history. For every defeat for one army, it is success for the opposing side. For centuries, men and women from across the globe have died or suffered severe injuries as they defend and protect in the name of their country.

In 1915, during World War I, 58,000 Allied soldiers died and 87,000 Ottoman Turkish troops died in a military disaster. Allied troops landed on an area of land called the Gallipoli peninsula on the modern-day Turkish coast.

Remembrance Day symbolizes the end of World War I and is an important opportunity to remember those who died in both world wars and other conflicts around the world.

THINK LIKE A WORLD WAR I SOLDIER

During World War I, German and British troops lived in trenches and showed each other no mercy—except on Christmas Day. Troops came out from the trenches and soldiers from both armies exchanged gifts and played soccer. When word of this informal truce reached commanders, the troops were threatened with punishment if they repeated such friendliness.

The Allied troops were sent to try to defeat the Ottoman troops, who were allies of the Germans. However, the men faced unexpected, fierce opposition. As the men fell, bodies rotted in the heat. Flies spread disease to the soldiers, who were surviving on limited water and food. The troops were pulled out in early 1916.

Battle of Gettysburg

In 1863, the Battle of Gettysburg ended the Confederate invasion of the North during the American Civil War. The Confederate Army outnumbered the Union forces. After three days of fighting, the Union troops overwhelmed the Confederates. The battle was a key turning point in the war but over three days, almost as many US soldiers died as did during the Vietnam War.

Remembrance Day poppy

Have You Got What It Takes?

Are you considering a career in the army? There are plenty of things you can start to do that will help prepare you for a military career.

School

Study hard and graduate. You need to have certain qualifications to join the army. For the US Army, you need a minimum of a High School Diploma or GED.

Consider Your Skills

Think about which specialization you would like to work in, such as combat, medicine, or communications. Consider what area would best suit your personality and skills.

Volunteer

Join clubs and groups that offer you the chance to improve your fitness and develop your team skills. How about mentoring or supporting a group of younger children in a particular sport? Take the opportunity to lead and support school friends. It will show the army your leadership qualities. Army roles often involve working with the community. Think about how you can help your local community, perhaps by offering to help raise funds for a local charity.

44

Fitness

It is essential you keep yourself in good physical shape. Take plenty of exercise and eat a healthy, balanced diet. Try out a range of exercises and make sure to include some team sports. Remember that an army always works as a team.

At Home

Talk to your parents or guardians about your plans. It helps to have their support.

Self Discipline

Keep your room and school books organized. This will help prepare you for the discipline and order needed to be in the army.

Personality

Make sure your behavior and actions are always responsible and thought through. The army seeks to recruit only young men and women who can live by its values.

ammunition the bullets used in guns

Army Reserve men and women who train for the army but keep their civilian jobs and may be called to action if there is a war

barracks where recruits live and train to join the army

civilians people not in the military

combat a fight, especially during a war

commissioned officer an officer who trains for a leadership role immediately

elite special and exclusive

enlisted members of the army who are not officers

evacuate to escape from a dangerous area

fortified protected

frontline close to the enemy

humanitarian looking after the needs of people

infantry soldiers who fight mainly on foot

marksmen soldiers skilled in precise shooting of targets

medic a soldier trained to give medical support

military to do with the armed forces

Modular Lightweight Load-Carrying Equipment (MOLLE) an army backpack

noncommissioned officer an officer who works their way up the army ranks

nuclear weapons bombs or missiles that use nuclear energy to cause incredibly destructive explosions

recruits people who have recently joined the military

routine a series of regular events

Taliban an extremist Islamic group

terrain land

terrorist a person who uses violence to force a government to change

tour of duty the length of time a soldier is engaged on a mission

For More Information

Books

Adams, Simon. *Soldier* (DK Eyewitness). New York,
NY: DK, 2009.

David, Jack. *United States Army* (Torque: Armed Forces).
Minneapolis, MN: Torque Books, 2015.

Doeden, Matt and Blake Hoena. *War in Afghanistan*
(You Choose: Modern History). North Mankato, MN:
Capstone Press, 2014.

Websites

Check out this website for a lot of information about working
for the US Army:
www.goarmy.com

For information on the key wars fought by the US Army
log on at:
www.ducksters.com/history

Have fun playing some army-related games at:
www.militarykidsconnect.dcoe.mil/tweens/games

Publisher's note to educators and parents: Our editors have carefully reviewed these
web sites to ensure that they are suitable for students. Many web sites change
frequently, however, and we cannot guarantee that a site's future contents will
continue to meet our high standards of quality and educational value. Be advised
that students should be closely supervised whenever they access the Internet.

Index